Coming Full Circle

Valerie Bridgeman Davis, Lana Book
Donna Woodard, Jim Walker

Edited by Susan Bright

Plain View Press
P.O. 33311
Austin, TX 78764

512-441-2452
sbpvp@eden.com

ISBN: 0-911051-85-6
Library of Congress Number: 96-069453
Copyright 1996, Plain View Press. All Rights Reserved.

Cover photograph taken in Port Aransas, Texas by Daryl Bright
Andrews.

Contents

Forward   5
Susan Bright

Icarus   6

I Bear Witness   9
Valerie Bridgeman Davis

The Poetry Council   9
Playing With the Boys   10
Root Mama   11
Come September   12
Southern Fried Memories   13
BadBoy Got Shot   14
For Your Mama   16
Fight   18
The Dream   19
I Bear Witness   20
Gran Gran Talks Fire
      Out My Hand   22
In Search of Warriors,
      Dark and Strong   25
Another Poem about Race   27
Dues Paid in Full   30
Grooming   32
A First in Many Ways   33
Seventeen Years Later   34
Going Crazy   35
Touch Me   36
Bone-deep Burning   37
Too Comfortable   38
When Mattie Belle
      Left Jimmy Lee   39

The Part That Counts   41
Lana Book

Casserole Ladies   42
Peanut Butter & Jelly   45
Don't Wash My Dishes!   46
S & H Green Stamps   48
Day Care   50

Aunt Dump   51
My Next 50   54
Dear Jane Fonda   55
Loyalty   56
I Know What Winter Feels Like 57
Minus Ten   58
Safe To Hate 59
Fences   60
Who Almost Was   61
De'Ja'Vu   62
Love in Room 403   63
Good Friday   65
Iced Tea   67

The Red Road   69
Donna Woodard

Waltzing Feet   70
Still Life With Vulture 72
Aslyum   73
Mamma's House   74
Filigree   76
Metronome   77
Fragile Fire   78
Brides in Waiting   79
Gentlest of Prisons   80
Embroideries   81
Radiant Flight   82
Sweet Surcease   83
Harbor Home   84
Niagara   85
Feast of Mourning   86
Swan   87
Angels Abounding   88
A Round . . .   89

Sudden Details   91
Jim Walker

Leaving   92
For A.   93
So Much, So Much, Oh . . .   94
The Birthday Trampoline   96
The Coach   97
As Much As Any Two People   98
Smoldering   100
Dinner Napkin as Icon   101
Memory Study 2   103
Listening to Poets   104
Weaving   105
After Living with Someone   107
Overture   109
As Regards   111
Regarding the Return of an Average Man 113

About the Writers   114

Foreword

by Susan Bright

As a poet and as the editor of Plain View Press I have had a great deal of listening to do. And parenting has required more of it. I listen to everything all the time. I listen for the meaning behind the meaning, for the magic spark of life, of hope. I listen for healing, for danger, to the song of the water as it flows over stones and to the hum of the computer. I listen to myself talking back to everything I hear.

I listen to the voices of writers as they begin the journey from idea to print, from voice to page. I listen to truths they unpeel from the core of life's sacred and scarred heart. I find incredible beauty in the process of listening to the work of new writers. Sometimes I listen to silence, which is also full and holy.

"Coming Full Circle" has grown out of an eighteen-month process of writing, rewriting, listening and performing. There have been periods of silence between work meetings. Writers joined the group and then dropped out creating pools of loss which our creative spirits had to fill. Creative process is unsettling. The people here dared to go on with their art when others gave up. They dared to wait for the vision to manifest, and their patience flowered. "Casserole Ladies," and "BadBoy Got Shot" came in at the last minute, as did the book title.

Our lives came together, spread apart and reformed. We each came full circle with the book. Our teenagers grew into and past urban catastrophe, a mom died, three daughters got married, jobs changed wildly, writers finished course work, went public with their poetry. Love kept being the answer, and patience. We insisted on beauty.

Until recently America has not listened to her poets. Now she needs us. She's pulled herself up from the frontier, moved in to the city, turned belly-up and now she is screaming. How could good ideas have become so corrupt? The poets are listening. They are telling her story. They are finding things to keep, things to change. They are inventing a better world.

Creative process is glorious, unpredictable and indominable. As this book goes to press, there are five others in the New Voices Series gathering momentum. Eve La Salle Caram is editing a West Coast fiction anthology in Los Angeles, Margo La Gattuta is working with writers in Michigan on a final edit of "Up From the Soles of our Feet," and I am reading for two publishing colonies and a Central Texas anthology.

At the source of all these books is the undeniable spirit of the writer, a voice which will not be stifled, an assurance that poets create meaning that is essential, that comes full circle.

Icarus

It didn't need a different ending—the story of a boy who flew up, with his father, to the Sun, the boy who invented wings to fly, dive through cloud cities, the boy who accomplished something impossible. That was before I had a son myself, when I was thinking of the self as primary, real, important, when invention was holy, like love, like fresh green water. Icarus appeared heroic—before my own son leaped too close to the diving board, ran into traffic, rode his bicycle into a train, rode it off a cliff into the river, drove the car, ran away. I spent years gasping as my child leaped head first into the air, knocked himself out, broke bones, flirted with oblivion, pulled his life out from under him, broke everything, broke me. Before a son came into my life, it didn't matter to me that Icarus fell out of the sky, awkward, like a new bird, fell to death, got swallowed up by the ocean, no one paying attention. I was in love with a vision, diamond cities below jet engines. Now I want the boy to live. I want him to reach for the sun and then come down—softly, like the angels that hover at his side, telling me everything will be alright. The way

Bruegel saw it is too cold for me—a gawkish thing tumbling out of the sky, people in the carnival, at the market, fishing, too busy to notice, or care. I want Icarus to come down alive, will not allow invention to cost so much. I have been trading teenager stories with friends who used to have different kinds of adventures (like the one who broke nineteen people out of a Mexican jail, for instance) with artists who have been inventing themselves from scratch since they grew into consciousness, with people on the edge whose hearts are wild—the ones who are the carnival, who create light, cut metal, carve stone, bend color to truth, sing. One eleven-year-old took the car, plowed down a row of new trees, and then took out the well. No water. Car totaled. Another boy shot a friend to death with his father's hunting rifle, by accident—overdoses, alcohol poisoning, car wrecks, gangsters, addiction, prostitution. Joe told me about a boy in Dallas whose father had a small airplane. Eleven-years-old, the boy snuck into the hanger, started the plane, drove it down the runway and took off—flew. Flew all over Dallas, circling, radioing the control tower, admitting he had no idea how to land. They had to close the airports, send incoming planes to Kansas, Alberqueque, Atlanta, Houston. For hours there was a maniac in the sky, circling the Dallas/Fort Worth metroplex. I imagine his parents, faces pressed against the sky like fish sucking aquarium glass, numb with terror. What happened is air control talked the boy down. It is so difficult today for kids. That's what we have to do. We have to talk them down.

○

I wrote this poem during the last months of the *"Coming Full Circle,"* workshop, when the book had another working title, before the last minute for changes. We seldom know we are coming full circle, or how to land. I offer it as a blessing for this new book.

Susan Bright
March, 1997
"Icarus," © Susan Bright, 1996.

I Bear Witness

The Poetry Council

We are all prophets,
telling the gospel truth,
we are all drinking
the nectar of the gods,

listening in on celestial
 conversations.

We gather, all of us,
using the same words
meaning different meanings
swirling, cavorting,
conjuring, dancing
with all these words,

asking each other, is this the truth?

All of us are on the party line
to the muses,
our pens, our tongues
dipped in the potions.

Some of us are rhyming,
some moving
to the beat of the drum,
working on the equations
for justice, love
and sex.

We are cursing evil,
and curing the disease
of desperate living
with our words, all of us.

Valerie
Bridgeman Davis

Playing With the Boys

When I was 12, my mother announced that
I had to stop playing football with the boys.
She said it wasn't ladylike, that I was budding.
She said, rolling around on the ground

with a group of boys on top of me
because I had the ball would give me a bad reputation,
the kind of reputation that follows girls into
dark alley-ways and gym floors and the
back seat of old cars, but not the kind
of reputation that makes nice boys
want to take you home to meet their baby sisters.

Well, I didn't then, and I don't now,
worry about my reputation
so that explanation didn't move me.
But I'm not the kind to argue
with my mother, that was my sister.

I didn't argue, but I did persuade the boys
to move the game from the backyard to the grassy knoll
just beyond the corn, because it didn't seem then,
it doesn't seem now, like a good idea
to stop playing with the boys.

Root Mama

Every new moon — thin slice, smiling sideways
and looking down on her — every new moon
found her walking
towards the woods,
mumbling mojo words
we never learned,
forgot to learn,
words we didn't know
at the time
we needed.

Every new moon Gran Gran walked, mumbling barely audible
power words from some forgotten tribe of Africa
healing words,
evil-preventin' words,
under her holy breath
walking toward
the woods.

Every new moon she left the house with a rag
that was never washed that I can remember —
a rag, and a ragged-edged knife
for cutting roots,
rooted exposure
rooted love
rooted health.

Every new moon, mumbling, walking, cutting roots
and blessing them for all our lives.
Roots we never learned,
forgot to learn,
roots we didn't know
at the time
we needed.

Come September

The year schools integrated
in Alabama, the last May
that all my classmates
and all my teachers
were black,
our U.S. history teacher
explained to us,

that come September,

even the smartest of us
would be the dumbest
in class
because
all the white children
were so much more
advanced,
smart,
prepared.

I spent the summer getting ready to be dumb.

He lied to us. I went back
to the business of excellence,
a venture come too late
for many of my ebony classmates
who dropped out in their minds
that last May
at one teacher's
explanation.

Southern Fried Memories

The last time we ate together,
        we were looking over a hot plate
                of southern fried catfish,
                        french fries
        and a cool glass
                of southern-sweetened tea.

And laughing, laughing hard
        because you
                were telling Eddie Murphy jokes
                better than Eddie.

And reminiscing, reminiscing over
        summer nights in Alabama
                with nine brothers,
                        one baby sister,
                and backwoods lynchings.

You were grinning over Jim Crow laws,
        and hooded neighbors,
                and laughing because, you said,
                        we got over in Alabama.

My catfish cooled and my tea warmed
        in your Deep South memories,
        and I stopped laughing
                because that wasn't the way
                I remembered
                        Alabama.

BadBoy Got Shot

BadBoy got shot.
It's a rumor, they say,
but a rumor from a source
close to the bullet.
14-years-old. Is he dead?
We're waiting for the
obituary to know.

Shot. He used to play in my house
with my sons; he was like my sons,
irritating, always hungry, and wrestling.
I'm a thousand miles away in Atlanta,
Chocolate City, where brothas drop
like bodies in a war zone
and body bags are disinfected
and recycled in 24 hours.

Oh, yeah, he was warned.
They were all warned. The football
teams, the basketball and track boys
in and out of my house, insistent, incessant.
"Hi Miss...... 'Bye Miss...... don't mind
me, Miss...... don't mind this bullet
in my stomach, my leg, my head."

BadBoy shot. I was always warning
that boy about his temper, telling him
to calm down, redirect his anger.
I kept saying, *You're gonna be somebody*
if you live to be 18, BadBoy.

Shot. And my sons are weeping inside,
scared, standing in that macho stance
teenagers get—arms crossed,
a glower flashing, baring their teeth,

14

sometimes. My sons are juiced
by their own need to be men,
testosterone kicking, growing pains,
late night wet dreams, and a mama
who does not want to know
what they wish for in the mornings.

So a thousand miles away,
I am wondering: where were all
the street angels? Where were
the alley angels? Where were they?
BadBoy shot. God help us all.

For Your Mama

I can't hate you, though I admit
I wanted to. I've tried to,
but I can't. Not because of you,
but because of her,

your mother, who sits
behind her door,
rocking back and forth
for you, worrying,

rocking on her knees,
stiff from repetition,
her face in her hands:

Dear Jesus, Oh God, Allah the Merciful, the Beneficent...

or your mother, pacing slowly
before a window,
looking out
longing for you....

where are you?

in her terry-cloth robe,
well into the mornings,
her head aching
from grief,

or your mother, numb from years
of your dog-wild life, wearing an
I-don't-care mask to keep from
losing her mind.

She has other children to protect.

Your mother volunteers
at the local elementary school,
looking for her little boy
in the crowd

needing to redeem herself, to forgive herself.
She remembers when you were nine,
and wrapped your arms
around her waist—

Mama, I love you best, you said.
*I 'll always be right here. I 'll
build a house next door when I 'm
grown and buy you the biggest
car there is.*

Your mother wants those arms again.

So, you killed my son, two of his friends,
and laughed while you reloaded,
smoking weed,
but I can't hate you.

I wanted to. God, how I wanted to.
But I can't. Because of her.

Fight

Bitch, he said.
Tonight, you gonna
put out, fight, or
hitchhike, and I
got out of the car,
started walking
miles from home,
or any lights.

We were deep
in backwoods country.
He could rape me,
kill me, I thought.
And no one would know
where to find me.
Terror covered me
like the darkness,
cloaking me with
a sickness that
reached my soul.

It was a football game
and a soda, I thought.
Not an invitation.
He drove off, kicking
gravel, hoping fear
would be an aphrodisiac,
making me yield.

Twenty minutes later,
he returned to that road
and saw me, walking
hard like an angry woman,
my nostrils flaring
with a righteous fire.
I had decided, it would be a fight.

The Dream

I am in the woods
behind the old homestead
a clearing
a cement-block house
like the one my grandfather built
except inside is not the chiffrobe
or iron beds I like so well
nor the buttermilk churn just inside
the backdoor porch,

but an asylum
and all the crazy people
grab me   through bars
where there should be chairs
and a wood-burning stove.

I go upstairs in a one-floor house   .
feeling, I don't know what,
and unable to see
the danger just ahead.

leave   wake up   walk away
I try.

The asylum people are free, and follow me
I run hard
again the people follow, walking
they catch up.

There is no escape from
secret family madness.

I tell the dream to my sisters,
who complete each scene
from a nightmare
of their own.

I Bear Witness

I bear witness
that we are a singin' people
a laughin' people
a move-your-hips-from-side-to-side people,

in churches and in bars
to the rhythm of our old worlds
in our new bodies
of pain and power.

I bear witness
that we are a renaissance people
an ancient people
an I've-got-my-family-in-me people,

all over the globe
a darker race
arising
from dusted goals.

I bear witness
that we are a prayin' people
a workin' people
a lifting-while-we-climb people,

in schools and in gyms
finding paths
and laying bricks
of hope and promise.

I bear witness
that we are a people
making it against odds together
and striving toward
a brand new way bearing
pressure, and our
lives
every
day.

Gran Gran Talks Fire Out My Hand

Stop that running, Children!

Ron, Esther, and me, sometimes Gwen, Red and Kevin
are running, playing tag, or whatever
game we have concocted.

We run back and forth, between the front yard and the back.
The house is a short cut to our fun;
a cast-iron bed brings a bruise to our knees.

Gran Gran's voice is rising with each trip we make through;
she pops the nearest bottom with a dishrag like a whip.

Stop that running Children, or I'll wring your necks,

and we all know she can because we've seen her in the yard
with a chicken by the neck; just another victim
of our Gran Gran's skill.

Stop that running, Children!

Scrambling, Ron pushes me on the way through their room
the only way through a little kitchen in the back
the only path to the porch,
and wood behind the shed.

Laughing, punching, playing, we all tumble
through the room, the heat thick because
Gran puts more coal in the stove.
Esther and I are falling and I reach to stop the fall
and land my hand in the center of the heat.

I told you to stop running!

She grabs me while I scream to high heavens

and my flesh is burning, I can hear it,
and Gran Gran is yelling,

Come here, and let me talk that fire out your hands!

One by one we stop and my cry becomes a whimper
We have all been here before:
running, burning, screaming,
and Gran Gran taking charge.

Each time she starts this way, fussing at the culprit.
Then calling forth her powers, she lifts the wounded part,
and intones like a mantra some shamanic words,

she shuts her eyes, starts humming some old Baptist tune
like on Sunday morning kneeling
summoning Spirit to the church,
the same song, the Original OM,
vibrating to bring the universe
into a unifying force.

I close my eyes and listen to her coax the burning pain
from the deep recesses it forges in my flesh,
fire running in my muscles, and boiling in my blood,
moving much too slow to escape fire-eating words.

Stop running, she must be saying,

making liquid heat retard and come backwards to her lips,
she breathes smoothing salve and potions,
each word a hunt for the soul of this fresh fire.

Come here, and stop running,

Gran Gran coos while I whine, and her lips are searing
from the fire in my fingers, and all of us are straining
to hear what she is saying, but we can only tell
that the words move in rhythm, rise and swell
intensifying with a command to fire
that must obey a wise old woman's words.

She assures there is no scarring, that her words have hit
their mark, and all signs of singe are finished,
and my hand is calm and cool.

Now, now, she says smiling, as we run back to our game.

In Search of Warriors, Dark and Strong

People, coarse
and unrelenting,
give over to the moment,
their dead selves
responding to a passionate,
riotous pain.
Death is in the street.

Vines are creeping over every wall,
under every bed,
stealing young souls
as they grow.

Drugs are our scourge.
Locate the source and cause.
And in the 'hood they are screaming
european-americans, gringos,
anglos, white people, white devils
and WHITE FOLK.

But there is a hole in the boat,
a poisonous vine in the streets.
Analyze its origin later.

Some fierce, strong African warriors
must plug the holes,
stand the stench,
staunch the wounds,
lay an ax to the root
to halt this tremulous growth,
its blood-filled floods.

Our Children are Dying.

My brothers are killing my sons.

People are stepping over
their bodies in memorial.

Some body find
a path
and lead us out.

Another Poem about Race

I am too sad to write another race poem;
to pontificate about our future in black and white;
to explain to my Jewish friends
why I wanted black men to go to D.C.,
Farrakhan notwithstanding.

I'm all for a million black men agreeing
to do the right thing.

I quit trying to explain why many of my brothers
ignored the Minister and his suspect motives
to join each other in repentance.

I was moved by speakers, by the voice of children,
old men dreaming dreams,
young men seeing visions.
I moved to embrace my sons, my brothers, fathers.
We need more BMWs—
Black Men Working, Black Men Weeping,
Black Men Making Worlds.

Did you hear the pledge?

I Will Not Hit My Wife.

I'm a black woman of the American South.
I've seen too many sisters nurse bruises
from loving the wrong man. I've cried
over women dead by the hands of spouses,
heads encaved, hearts imploded
because there is no room for the lover's rage
except inside her head.

I Will Not Abuse My Daughters
Or My Sons.

There will be no more crying when a father beats his son
because he sees too much of himself in the boy,
beats him with a cord, a bat, a board, beats him
until the child learns to hate the hand that feeds him.

I Will Not Lift My Hand In Violence
Against Anyone. I Will Not
Abuse My Body.

My brothers will no longer crack up,
needle their veins, fire their brains.

I Will Work.

We're not asking anybody for anything.
We came to repent and take responsibility
for the children we have fathered,
the violence we have engendered
the drugs we have perpetuated,
the women we have pimped.

Who among you will argue with these promises?

Explain to me why the same America
that calls black men shiftless and lazy
were angry when those men said, *you're right.*
We've waited for our wives, our lovers,
our mothers, our sisters, our daughters,
our government to do for us.
No more. We're awake. We will do it.

There has been enough talk, too many meetings.
There is too much work to do
to let a whole race die in committee.

Is this same America scared, or just angry
because:

        Mainstream America is not orchestrating
        the next black messiah?
        Blacks are no longer waiting
        for America's approval rating?
        Betty Shabbazz hugged Louis Farrakhan?
        Black people will forgive the worst of sins
        for the sake of survival?

Dues Paid in Full

I know the power of racial hatred,
      pay my dues
            to be black
                  and female
                        in America.

I have my credentials ques-tion-ed,
my intelligence scrut-i-niz-ed,
my loyalties test-ed.

I work hardER, longER,
      cry for my children,
            fight for my husband,
                  lose friends
because I am too black,
questionably black,
not black enough.

I get angry when I'm followed in a store,
stopped for no reason,
tomatoed,
spit at,
stoned.

I'm called alternately radical and oreo,
pushy and sell-out,
too race-sensitive,
too mulatto.

I have no belief in black unity at all costs,
      at all compromises,
            no patience for people
                  yelling *Uncle Tom* at me
                      because I am not
                          angry enough.

I'm weary at being told, *You're not like other blacks*,
by whites who think they like me,
puzzled, since they do not like blacks,
in principle.

I am tired of blacks who do not
sanction my ability to navigate
dangerous waters of two worlds
                    or my use of
                            Queen's English
                                    or my knowledge of
                                    Shakespeare and Maya,
                                            Verdi and Marsalis.

I have no desire to be white.
I am tired of having to prove I'm black.
I no longer want to bear the burden
for all blacks everywhere
a requirement America demands
of me and every child of Africa.

Grooming

Your mother tells me
        you disappear for days
                into darkness of night
to she-does-not-know-where.

She tells me
        while she combs
                your daughter's hair,
springy and warring against the comb.

She tells me, your mother,
        that darkness claims you,
                making you irrational,
                        irresponsible,
                        wild.

Be still, your mother says to your daughter,
        and tenderly jerks your daughter's head
                to enforce her command.

I watch, knowing
        your mother means these *be still* words
                for you.

You disappear darker than darkness
        which claims you for nights into days,
                your dark blood, purple-red,
runs first through your longing mother,
        now through your ancient daughter.

I listen as your mother tells me
        you could never *be still*.

A First in Many Ways

This is my body given for you. . . .

At 12, Janay decided to love him.
Three years later, she offered him her body.
She lay down on his bed when her parents
were away, and said, *I'm yours.*

He was 16 then, and though he said he had,
he had never been with a girl and his sex
in the room at the same time.

She took his left hand in both of hers,
and pulled her body next to him.
She wore a slip dress to make it easy.
She had planned every detail.

She guided his hand to her breast,
then kissed him, hot and wet.
She did not have to guide him again,
except to slow him down.

It was a first in many ways.
He ached afterwards, sent her away,
he wanted to be alone with his memories.

She thought he hated her
when he said nothing,
and would not even
watch her leave.

On the contrary,
he was afraid
he would never love
anyone but her.

Seventeen Years Later

Seventeen years is a long time
to go without speaking to the woman
who brought you into this world.

Forty-nine hours of labor,
then laid up recovering,
and nursing for another six weeks.

It was the last time you hugged me seriously.

Every time afterwards, you acted
as if it pained you, or at least
irritated you to touch me.

You grimaced every time
a neighbor noted our resemblance.

Now, you're laying on a bed—
not recovering—and a Hospice nurse
has called to say that

in less than forty-eight hours
I must speak to you
for the first time
in seventeen years,
or I will never have the chance
to hold you dearly.

Mothers should not die
before their daughters
are ready to forgive them.

Going Crazy

It didn't take long to go crazy, really.
She was already leaning edgeward,
waiting for someone to call to her,
but she didn't know who.

And it was a short drop upward, crazy.
She could not find the handle,
civilized as she was, for so long clear
about how to get around in a world
where men and babies require
the same kind of attention.

When she decided it was time,
she donned a shawl from her
great-grandmother's closet,
so she could go *properly* crazy.
Called the children to her side,
kissed them all *hello*, told them to
take care of their father—
he would never understand,

but she had to go now, or the barge
would leave without her and she didn't know
when another one would come,
crazy being a journey
many people want to take,
so the boat is
always
full.

Touch Me

For Don

Run your hungry hands
along my tender legs.
Touch me gently
in my place of knowing.

Rest your finger tips,
here, in the small
of my back,

let me feel your breath
permanent on my neck,
sense your power hard
against my body.

Lay your chocolate-coated body
next to mine, fill my nostrils
with your scent, pour
an offering of your love,
a libation on my
waiting ground.

Touch me,
deep and eternal.

Bone-deep Burning

I wrapped myself in sheets tonight
trying to stop myself from longing,
coming to you.

My body rages against all reason
        howling into the torrent of fire
                that is the fervor of your touch,
                        the heat from it burning all
bridges to sanity, luring me on.

I am feverish,
sick really, with passion.

My body screams against all sense
        yelling into the cascade of desire
                that is the zeal of your press,
                        the power from it collapsing all
determinations to soberness.

And the fire burns in my bones,
singeing my heart, but not enough
to make me draw away
from the flames.

Too Comfortable

The day comes
when the comfort sets in,
and you know where the socks go
finally;
and which drawer
to stick his drawers in,
and when to cook pot roast;
and which football game
not to talk through.

And you figure out
when to call his mother,
where to park the car,
which after shave smells good on him
even if he doesn't know it;
and which of his friends are dogs,
but he likes them anyway,
and which friends of his
you like way too much,
so you stay away. ·

And you know
when to buy new shirts,
where to buy tickets to the show,
who his favorite fighter is,
when to hush the kids.

And the day comes
when you sit down and cry
from all the comfort.

When Mattie Belle Left Jimmy Lee

Child, Mattie Belle just went crazy.
Crazy, I tell you.
She just lost her mind.

There she was married,
washing Jimmy Lee's shirts,
and all.
With his children, too, you know.
I mean *kids*.

They don't know.
Mattie Belle, she religious, too.
Are you listening to me?

There she was,
cooking, they say.
Just walked out the door
one day.
Out the door,
that's what they tell me.

Who knows what was in her mind
when she left rice cooking
on the stove—and no note.
God!
I can't even tell.
She was always
so *practical*.
She always
left
a
note.

Lana Book

The Part That Counts

I live at *The Hill Country Sculpture and Meditation Garden*. The buildings are constructed from one hundred year old pine beams that Willie put up alone using a come-along. The level and yard stick were thrown away years ago. The walls curve. The roof goes up and down and up again. Stone and mortar hold it all together. Magical creatures peak through antique windows and hang from hand carved woodwork. Wild cherry and walnut trees stretch above the oaks surrounding the box canyon we live in. The scent of cedar mingles with sage, rosemary, curry and garden phlox along wooded paths. At night the crickets sound like bells on the ankles of native people that once camped near the creek. By the campfire at night, as Willie and I stargaze, he reminds me that this is the good part, the part that counts.

Casserole Ladies

Tears rolled down Helen's face as she chopped the big purple onion. When the phone rang, she knew it was Sophie. Sophie called every Sunday morning after reading the obituaries.

"Helen, have you read the obits yet?"

"Yes, Louise Kemper, God rest her soul," Helen answered as she stirred the chopped onion and minced garlic into the hot olive oil.

"Survived by her loving husband, Theodore Kemper. I'm making chicken in red wine sauce for this one, Helen. Pick you up at two-thirty."

Helen got out her blue china casserole dish. A disposable foil would be more convenient but then there would be no need for it's return. It was an important strategy she learned from Sophie. She taped labels with her name, address, and phone number on the bottom of the blue dish and inside the lid then put the spaghetti casserole in the oven to stay warm until Sophie arrived.

Sophie knocked on her door at exactly two-thirty. "Timing is crucial, Helen. One day too early and you're too aggressive. One day too late and you're beat out by the competition."

"Sophie, I've been widowed by two husbands. I'm not looking for another one."

"Nonsense. What are you going to do with the rest of your life? Play bridge once a week and sit alone in this big house waiting for your children to make their token visits twice a year? We're still young, Helen, barely sixty-five. We've paid our dues over the years. Life owes us a little fun and companionship toward the end."

Helen put her spaghetti casserole in the styrofoam chest in the back seat next to Sophie's chicken with wine sauce. Sophie checked the address in the paper before starting the car.

"It's on the other side of town. We'll have to use the freeway."

"Maybe we should take the streets through down town."

"The traffic is even worse down town," Sophie said as she backed out the driveway.

"Sophie, doesn't this seem a little premeditated? I mean, aren't we taking advantage of a man when he is most vulnerable? When he is still grieving for his wife? We hardly knew Louise Kemper."

"It isn't premeditated. It's planned. There's a difference. For Christ's sake, Helen. We aren't the CIA on a covert mission. We're just two old ladies paying our respects. Delivering casseroles and condolences. Besides, he may be grieving now but give him six months and he'll have a sweet thing half his age on his arm. How many times have you seen that happen?"

"A few I guess."

"More than a few I'd say. Look at Murry Gletz. Doris wasn't in her grave a year when he married that red head. She can't be more than forty. Now she's eating off Doris' china, sleeping in Doris' bed and he's had two heart attacks. The old fool."

Sophie slowly eased into the traffic of the freeway as cars backed up and honked behind her.

"I told you we should have driven through down town," said Helen.

"I know how to drive, Helen. I didn't spend two hours making that casserole to have it end up all over my back seat because some jerk is in a hurry. Just watch for our exit."

They drove in silence until they reached the Windsor Blvd. exit. Sophie pulled off the exit ramp and turned right. "It shouldn't be much further," she said.

"Don't you think it's funny, Sophie, when a man dies and leaves a spouse she is suddenly a threat to the wives of couples she has known for years. The invitations stop and she becomes socially isolated. But when a woman dies and leaves a spouse he immediately becomes fair game, available, desired at every social function in town. It seems to me, society supports the widower and pities the widow. It isn't fair. Aren't you and I just perpetuating that behavior?"

Sophie stopped the car in front of a red brick house. The sign above the mailbox read, 621 Windsor Blvd., The Kempers.

" I can't believe you're this age and still expect life to be fair. We aren't perpetuating anything. We didn't make the rules, Helen. The way I see it, we're just adding balance to the scale."

Helen and Sophie walked toward the house carrying their casseroles.

"I don't know why I keep coming with you," said Helen.

"You keep coming with me because you know

I'm right. Because, like me, you're tired of being alone. Because the silence makes you crazy. Because you lie in your bed alone and can't remember what it feels like to be touched. Now, how do I look?"

"Lose the smile, Sophie. It doesn't look sincere," Helen said as she rang the door bell.

Peanut Butter & Jelly

She used to say
she wished she had a dollar
for every time she spread
peanut butter and jelly
between slices of bread,
wrapped it in waxed paper,
carefully laid it
in the brown bag
on top of the apple and carrot sticks
so it wouldn't get mashed,
dropped in a dime for milk
and a note that said
I love you,
watched the child
dash through the kitchen,
grab the bag,
stuff it in his coat pocket
as he ran out the door.
Now, every morning she sits
alone at her kitchen table
until the school bus
passes her house, listening
to the man on the radio recite
the school lunch menus and
wonders why the smell of peanut butter
still makes her cry.

Don't Wash My Dishes!

Georgia says I have no decorating theme, and that I should sell most of what I have and get one, maybe Early American or Oriental. "So what," I say. "I live alone with a cat, so why do I need a theme?"

"Look, you have a modern, thousand dollar, angular sofa sitting next to a round, thirty-five dollar chair covered in black Naugahyde from the fifties. Doesn't that tell you something?"

"Yeah, I got a damn good deal on the chair."

I can always tell when Georgia is getting exasperated. She puts her hands on her hips, the veins in her neck bulge out, and she looks at me like a calf staring at a new gate.

"For God's sake," she says to me, "you have a pink Buddha sitting in the window and your mother's blue glass and ivory crucifix hanging over it. Your mother would just die. It's sacrilegious! You probably don't even go to Mass anymore."

"She won't care. She's already dead," I say. I decide not to tell her about Sufi dancing on Sunday. Enough is enough.

Georgia sees her mother's face every time she looks in the mirror. I tell her she sounds more like the old woman every day. "You know you will never please her. She criticizes you constantly. Give it up. It's too late. It isn't healthy," I tell her.

"I love my mother. She's a saint," she says. Better hers than mine is what I say.

"Well, what would your children say if they saw all those 'danglie' things hanging from the ceiling over your bed and chili pepper lights around the window?"

"They already have. They were jealous."

"You live like a Bohemian. You only wash dishes once a week. It's embarrassing. What's all this stuff for anyway?" she wants to know.

"It's romantic," I say.

"Romantic? Are you crazy? You're over fifty years old. Don't you know there's a epidemic out there?"

Georgia has been my friend for more than twenty years, and together we have weathered the storms of divorce and raising children, but she has always been secretive about her relationships. It bothers me. She says she hasn't met a man yet who can do more for her than she can do for herself, and that includes sex. I tell her she's been meeting the wrong men.

Sure we have our differences, but I admire her sense of organization. All of her dishes and towels match, and every room in her house flows ritually into the next. She has a theme.

It's not that she really wants to change me. Not really. She just sees a part of me in herself that scares her. Once she even told me she admired my free spirit. She said she wished she could wear heels without stockings and dresses that show some cleavage. "But it isn't right," she says. "At our age we have to be careful."

She worries about me. She wants to know what I'm going to do when I get old and how will I live. She says that I'm the only person she knows who pays twenty-five dollars for a print and two hundred to frame it, and insists on buying hard backs instead of paperbacks.

"I'm saving every cent I can so I can enjoy life when I get old," she says. So I remind her she turned sixty last November. "Well don't come begging to me when they throw you out on the street without a penny and no insurance."

She doesn't mean it though. We have shared loyalty. Just before my second divorce we sneaked into my husband's office at midnight. Georgia stood watch at the door while I ransacked his desk looking for financial statements. And there was the time I stayed with her in the hospital when she had breast implant surgery, and lied to her children about it when she asked me to because she didn't want them to know.

We were something back then. Fearless and defiant. She was fearless, and I was defiant. It's kept us bonded over the years. So even though she says my lifestyle makes her crazy, she thinks I'm fun to be with. And even though her obsessive compulsive behavior is irritating, I still let her wash my dishes when she comes to visit.

S & H Green Stamps

The first time Frank met Delores
he figured her for a hard sell.
He knew these things from instinct
being a crackerjack salesman for the
R.L. Watkins Co., he had hustled products
from Cleveland to New Jersey
since he was sixteen.
His experience told him it was only
a matter of packaging and presentation.

The first time Frank proposed
he dressed in his pin stripe,
shined his wing tips,
donned his new fedora,
brought her two bottles of vanilla,
and a bottle of emulsified coconut
oil shampoo from his sample case.

Delores wasn't impressed.

By his third proposal,
sensing he was losing ground,
Frank made his last pitch for Delores.
He promised he would settle down,
buy a house,
get a job at the local I.G.A.,
go to church,
and just because he loved her,
he would throw in ten filled
books of S & H Green Stamps.

Delores accepted.

Thirty years later Delores
said Frank had her hooked
from the beginning.
Frank believes it was the
S & H Green Stamps that
finally won her over.
He said, "Keep your foot
in the door and offer them
something for free. It's a
sure sale every time."

Day Care

Mother doesn't notice the
clock on her dresser has
been blinking for three years.
Time isn't relevant now.
A women who once made a
Thanksgiving dinner for twelve
look easy, shuffles through her
kitchen holding onto chair backs
and counters,
  forgets to turn the gas off,
  forgets to eat.

Meals on Wheels delivers
foil covered lunches she feeds
to the cats that gather
at her back door.
She keeps the shades pulled
because she says
the neighbors are communist.

"You will like this place.
You won't be alone.
They offer hot meals, a place
to nap, birthday parties, bingo,
nurses, and high toilet seats."
But she's worried she won't be there
when her children get home from school.
I reassure her,
  tell her I love her,
  tell her I'll be back at five.
She grips my arm and whispers,
"Honey, have you seen my daughter here?"

Aunt Dump

"Ella Mae Chew is too high spirited and head strong for a woman," her sister, Rosa, would often say. She was my great aunt on my father's side. Everyone called her Dump, except for the children who called her Aunt Dump. The Dump name came from her round, squatty stature. I was taller than her in the sixth grade, a fact I never mentioned out of respect and fear. One evening when I was about ten, while the two of us sat by the fireplace in the two room log cabin where she was raised, Aunt Dump told me she was the widow of Lonnie Burnett, an outlaw from Gonzales County.

"I was charmed by his wit and good looks. I married him when I was eighteen, then left him and moved back home after two years when our baby, Emily, died. He came back for me one time you know, but Papa ran him off with a shotgun. Lonnie was too wild, but I loved him passionately. Not long after that he was killed trying to rob a store," she said in a whisper, her voice quivering, as she shared the most intimate part of her life with me.

The family never talked about Aunt Dump's marriage or the death of her infant daughter but there was always a sorrow when she spoke of them to me. She never remarried, never had much good to say about any man after that.

Aunt Dump and Rosa left their home at Cheapside, in DeWitt County, after the drought in the fifties. When the cattle were sold at auction she moved from relative to relative. "Just visiting," she would say. The land was leased to another rancher and Aunt Dump settled at Smiley in a three-room remodeled structure that was once Mrs. Bundick's chicken house.

I could always count on her bringing lemon drops and Dentyne gum when she visited our family. When we bought our first television, Aunt Dump would sit in the living room with us, holding a newspaper between her face and the screen to protect herself from the rays. If Mama let me I would go with her when she left to keep her company for a few days.

On our way to her house, we sometimes stopped at a road side stand and bought Dewberries for a dollar a gallon. Aunt Dump made steaming cobblers and green grape pies on a wood stove. "The secret is to pour fresh cream through slits in the crust as soon as they're done," she said, moving them from oven to table as if she were handling fine bone china. Streams of lavender sweat ran down her face. "I put a fresh wrench in my hair yesterday," she said, dabbing her forehead with a dish towel.

Winter nights we slept together under hand made feather quilts that protected us from the cold wind whistling through cracks around windows and doors. I sunk into our nocturnal cocoon feeling secure, knowing her loaded forty-five pistol was under the bottom feather mattress.

Aunt Dump never seemed to change. Even as a child I admired her gutsy determination and unwavering honesty. Those snappish black eyes could devour anyone who tried to tell her what to do. My mother thought she was too arrogant for a woman. My father never questioned her. I remember her hair was always tightly curled, wiry, the color of lilacs. Dark skin and eyes black as Buckeye seeds. "It's the French in me," she would say. She smelled of talc powder and snuff that would run down the crevices from the corners of her mouth to her chin. I could feel the stiff ribbed corset she wore daily beneath her crisp starched dresses when I hugged her. She never wore pants. "Ain't ladylike," she said.

Aunt Dump saw my Catholic upbringing as paganism and appointed herself guardian of my soul. Once a month, when the Pilgrim Presbyterian Church had a minister, I would see her racing up the dirt road to our house, a cloud of dust billowing from behind her fifty-two Chevy, to take me to Sunday services. We sat next to each other, cooling ourselves with paper fans, Jesus's picture on one side, an advertisement for the hardware store on the other.

After services, it was her custom to visit the cemetery with her old friends, Nita Keaney and Tot Plowman. The three women shared a common history. They had been independent ranch women who survived the hardships of working the land and cattle alone in a era dominated by men. I recall her saying, "Nita can work cattle better than any man but she still dresses proper for church. Tot never wore a dress in her life. I gave her a pink chintz once and she cut it up and pieced it in a quilt." I remember Aunt Dump walking among the headstones mumbling to herself, roaming over thousands of mental acres of her past, bending to caress the ground over those she cherished.

Aunt Dump lived a hundred years. She's buried at Pilgrim Cemetery under a huge Oak, her sister, Rosa, on one side, and her infant daughter, Emily, on the other. Now, as I touch the cool pink granite above her grave, I understand what these people and this place meant to her. Here, where birds sing to the morning's rising sun from their nests in the tall trees, deer feed on the tender meadow grass at dusk, and fireflies light the paths at night, she was akin to the splendor of dawning and the stillness of sunsets.

My Next 50

I'll live grandly
my next 50 years:
take out a second mortgage,
get a gold VISA,
travel to Pago Pago,
lie naked in the sun
with bronze colored natives,
sip rum from a pineapple,
watch sweat trickle down
hard muscles.
And when the children ask
where I have been,
I'll lie and say,
"A senior citizen tour
to visit the Pope."

I'll cash in the life insurance,
buy diamonds and chiffon dresses
with plunging necklines
I'll wear to Safeway,
eat giant shrimp by the pound
and the freshest pastries,
find my Gloria Swanson cigarette holder,
and start smoking again,
use my best crystal to drink
the finest brandy and champagne
until the sun rises.
And when the children ask
about their inheritance,
I'll lie and say, "Not to worry,
it's been taken care of."

Dear Jane Fonda

Dear Jane, I send this S.O.S.
My body gone, my life a mess.
I've read the books and watched
your tape.
I'm under tall and overweight.
I'm in a metabolic slump
even though I pump and pump.

Creams and gels and silicone?
My breast have shrunk, my hips
have grown.
Even though I herbal wrap,
my *abs* organically overlap.
A fortune spent on liposuction—
I aimed for total reconstruction.
When I awoke I wasn't thin,
they didn't remove it—
they put more in.
Too late, I found to my surprise
that cellulite solidifies.
I diet on carrots and lettuce leaves,
measuring that and weighing these.
How did it all get so chaotic?
I'm a Nutri System neurotic.

I'm desperate Jane.
Please send advice by express mail.

Loyalty

He's fifty-two and worries
about his declining libido,
so just in case...
he keeps a woman on the side for Tuesday afternoons,
and makes love to his wife once a week.

She's forty-nine and wonders
if she is still attractive,
so just in case...
she sees another man from two to four on Fridays,
and makes love to her husband once a week.

He thinks she needs a vacation,
and she thinks he needs counseling,
so just in case...
they both agree. Because Lord knows they're loyal,
the question is to whom?

I Know What Winter Feels Like

Your words no longer make me flinch,
I hear them garbled, distant.
If I say you're forgiven,
will that make you happy?
I need time to rehearse that kind of generosity.
A litany of your future without me
does not command my attention.
My days have quit dividing
into before and after.
I will admit some nights I laid awake,
watching my endings crash into my beginnings,
like a frigid gray solstice.
But as a seed sprouts and pushes
through earth's darkness toward sunlight,
I chose life's spring and summer,
because I know what winter feels like.

Minus Ten

After all,
      he loved her ninety percent and
      thought she was a fool for giving a hundred.

Let's face it,
      a man should reserve ten percent just
      in case something better comes along.

      It's at least prudent.

Poor man,
      never did understand
      why she wasn't grateful.

So now,
      he's ninety percent alone and ten percent crazy
      living with the presence of her absence,
      because she's one hundred percent gone.

Safe To Hate

My first memory
is hating that tree,
the one that grew
twenty feet tall, lean
with a pointed top.
I remember
the fury of a three year old,
consciously, determinedly,
standing with clenched fists,
tight jaw,
eyes shooting fire
to sear its core,
wishing it dead.

My desire, my obsession,
was to carve words of rage
deep into it's trunk,
scream so loud
it trembled, and
every leaf fell,
leaving it naked,
exposed, vulnerable.
I wanted to
cut it to the ground,
hear it moan with
each swing of my ax,
watch it's juice run like tears.

Fences

Barbed wire stretched taut between posts,
cedar stripped clean, staggered zig zag,
stone cut square, mortared geometrically,
broken down weathered fences
say the same thing:
there are many ways to keep people
out of your life.
Political fences, holy wars.
Atrocities rage in God's name,
neighbor kills neighbor,
children die.
Mothers in Israel or Sarajevo will tell you.
Fences with signs warning
no trespassing, private property, keep out.
We stand on the other side
longing for greener grass.
Remember, weeds look good from a distance.
Children cloistered behind fences of apathy
struggle against failure.
Even white picket can tear your heart out.

Who Almost Was

Everytime I lose someone
I grieve for everyone I've
lost all over again.

People warm and gentle,
who loved me without motives,
let me love them without being afraid.

I grieve for some that didn't,
those I've spent time with that couldn't stay,
and disappeared before I was able to let them go.

Sometimes it's easier to lose someone
who has been a part of my life,
than it is to lose someone who almost was.

De'Ja'Vu

I don't know when I quit waiting,
only how it felt:
glass shattering in slow motion,
time cutting through me
grain by grain
severed connections.

I remember rose petals
in an alabaster box,
and the scent of the bed
after you left it.
You said you would call soon,
de'ja'vu.

Love in Room 403

"Shh...", she whispered, putting one finger to her lips as she rose from the fold-away bed when I entered the room. She leaned over the familiar body, her hands lingering here and there, as if to reassure herself he was still alive. Recognizing her touch, he did not startle, but reached to stroke her cheek, his movement weak and shaky, then opened his eyes.

"I've never been away from Henry for one night, and I'm not going to start now," Grace told me as she held his hand. I saw the magic between them as they looked at each other, that sparkle of youthful love in geriatric bodies. There was no embarrassment or awkwardness in their display of affection for one another.

Grace left the room then returned with a cup of coffee for Henry. "We've been together over sixty years, and Grace has brought a cup of coffee to my bed every morning since we were married," Henry said, gasping for air between each sentence. Their eyes never moving from each other, they continued to talk about their years together as if they were alone.

"Henry, do you remember the trip we took to Mirror Lake? Wasn't it 1939?"

"Yes, dear, I believe it was. I was afraid the old Ford wouldn't make it through the mountains."

"Remember the owner of the cabins brought us a string of fish? You didn't want to clean them and I didn't want to eat them, so we buried them behind the cabin after dark."

Henry and Grace were surrounded by a warm glow, separating them from the aseptic starkness of the hospital room. I knew I was experiencing something rare.

"Oh, I know I've spoiled him over the years, but we were never blessed with children, so I've nurtured him like a child," Grace said, as she straightened his pillow and adjusted the oxygen cannula on his face.

Henry's condition worsened by evening. His breathing became shallow and he could no longer respond to Grace's voice or touch. I wondered if he would survive the night.

When I arrived the next morning, Henry was lying flat in bed, the oxygen had been removed, the sheet neatly tucked around him. Grace was sitting at his bedside.

"You know, Henry was always in charge," she said. "I never questioned him. But he finally did something I told him to. I said Henry, it's time to rest now. I'm going to be okay. Close your eyes and go to sleep. Then he just laid back and he was gone."

"Grace, can I call someone to be with you?" I asked.

"No dear, there is no one, just Henry and I," she said.

I stayed with Grace while she gathered his belongings, watching her caress every item as she packed them in Henry's suitcase. She stood at his bedside, and with trembling hands removed the gold band from his ring finger, then leaned over him and kissed his cheek. I put my arms around her and for the first time she cried. Grace looked at me, her eyes asking questions she knew I had no answers for.

"What do I do now, just leave him here?"

How do you ask someone to entrust their companion of sixty years to you? How do you tell them it's time to let go, that their role has ended?

"Yes, Grace," I said. "I'll take care of things."

She picked up the suitcase, and I watched her walk away, alone.

Good Friday

Friday, April 14, 1995
4:30 P.M.

The black rosary she always keeps in bed is lying beneath her cold, limp hands, some of the black worn from the large wooden beads. A priest in Bethlehem had given her that rosary years ago.

I pull back the sheet. Mary is unresponsive as I touch her and call her name. Her blue eyes are open, fixed, the pupils constricted. Only shallow respirations through her gaping mouth and a faint irregular pulse tell me she is still alive. Her head extended backwards, neck stretched, I reach and straighten it as if it would make her more comfortable.

A white rosary is wrapped around her left wrist. A scapula hangs around her neck. A small square piece of cloth on a black cord remains, the saint's picture long since worn away.

As I pull up the sheet, lean over to stroke her slightly warm forehead and soft white hair, I recall a story she told me. Her parents died when she was a small child and she was sent to live in a Catholic orphanage. One day Sister Elizabeth was going to cut all the girl's hair, including Mary's long blond braids. The priest there wouldn't allow her to cut Mary's hair because he thought it was so beautiful. She said they continued to be friends for years.

Last week, as she slipped in and out of coherency, three priests visited her at different times to give her the anointing of the sick. Mary dismissed each one from her room saying she would wait for Father Mike, the priest from her childhood who had saved her blond braids.

5:00 P.M.
I'm checking on Mary again. Her breathing has slowed. I can barely feel her pulse now. Her feet and legs are mottled. On her bedside table are four small statues of saints she has carefully wrapped in embroidered hankies, and placed in a rusting cookie tin, three neatly folded yellowing pillow cases with hand crocheted edges, a St. Christopher medal, and holy water in an old bottle

marked Lourdes Water.

Yesterday Mary was sitting in a recliner in the hall with the holy water bottle gripped tightly in one hand. She was talking to God and Angels and as each one of us passed she poured some water in her other hand and gave her blessing as she sprinkled us. I unscrew the cap, put some holy water on my finger, and make the sign of a cross on her forehead whispering, "*In nomine Patris, et Filii, et Spiritus Sanctus*, God bless you too Mary."

There is a time just before death, a space between this life and the next, where the spirit seems to be hovering, waiting for the last heartbeat to set it free. I wonder where she is now? I want to know if what she is experiencing is more beautiful and meaningful than all of her past eighty-one years. I want her to tell me what it is like, to die I mean.

Iced Tea

I've been angry since July, 1958, ever since Mr. Fred came to help my papa work cattle. Every summer for two scorching weeks he helped brand and treat the cattle for screw worms. Twenty men sat at our table every day for lunch, except for Mr. Fred who was always last in line. He filled his plate with chicken, corn, potatoes, dipped water from the well with a metal cup that hung from his belt and sat outside under a mesquite tree to eat alone.

When I asked Mama why Mr. Fred didn't take iced tea she said, "Well water's good enough." When I asked Papa why Mr. Fred didn't eat at the table with the other men he didn't say a word. His hands closed in fists around his fork and knife and he gave me that look that said, "Shut up girl." Mama turned her back, pretending she hadn't heard.

I slipped out the back door with a glass of iced tea for Mr. Fred. When Papa found me, he dragged me back to the house, thrashing me with a mesquite switch, all the way yelling, "You don't be mingling with no black men, girl. I won't have folks thinking I raised no heathen child." I could see tears in Mr. Fred's eyes. But I didn't cry. I was angry.

I returned home for the first time in twenty years after Papa died last summer. As everyone gathered at Mama's house for lunch following the services, I could see Mr. Fred standing under that tree. When he saw me walking toward him with two glasses of iced tea, tears filled his eyes. We sat together under that old mesquite tree all afternoon just sipping our iced tea, and decided that after forty years we wouldn't be angry anymore.

The Red Road

Donna Woodard

Native Americans call it, "traveling the Red Road", i.e. the high road in life, the need to know oneself before all others. Writing keeps me on that road— it is as essential as breathing and as familiar and terrifying as looking in a mirror and seeing the whole of who I am. I've often felt that writers write because they are pursued by demons but also because they are surrounded by angels. The process itself is a weaving which becomes a tapestry which becomes a part of who I am, a part of my "Red Road."

Waltzing Feet

I love my mother—
her Belafonte records
and waltzing feet
her sharpshooter's eye and precise diction.
It is her German heritage you understand.
Her tiny waist and seashell belt.
I sang Italian at three
and she calmly looked on nodding—
"you see?"

I love my mother and bleed for her.
I'm jealous of those others who knew her first.
I was too great a price to pay.
But somewhere far back
when her first love sang
 "Jeannie with the Light Brown Hair"
while ripping out her heart
she decided to grow those sons and daughters
as steady as the strongest song to cultivate
the cadence that sang forth from me.

Her tears were never hidden good enough
from my inquisitive eye.
They dragged me to the bottom.
But she stayed.

I love my mother.
I made her promise never to leave me,
to die by my side, to be with me always,
to wait as I grew.

I sit on her bed, the one she bequeathed to me
and imagine years from now lying within its wooden arms
on quilts she stitched in rooms she graced
with words she placed in my very heart.

Can I do this thing? Will I still see angels?

Still Life With Vulture

"*I die*" you say and smile that smile
reeking of faint lunacies and Van Gogh dreams,
tobacco-stained fingers hovering among the jewels —
a Vulture

waiting to descend. "*I die*" you say, poised for reply,
sarcastic smirk, the knife's edge already beginning
to cleave the loaf.
Ruins,

the spilling of the wine, rivulets among my mind.
Your words are dread shrouded and even deeper gloom,
but come at last with the finish of a painted glaze,
aburst, aflame, one meager moment of madness
and then, the lessening, dulling quietness of a
Death

long coming, eager in its conclusion, greedy in its demise
looking upward toward the longed for
birth.

Aslyum

Mother leads you out across the lawn,
the manicured lawn.
No paint-chipped chairs or windblown trash,
just empty order, empty steps.
We speak of unimportant things — the weather and the flowers,
careful not to give you time to answer back — as if you even would.
You are so still, so supervised and straight,
ringless fingers, distant eyes.
My mother cries and fingers a greasy picnic lunch.
My father stands a distance off and studies clouds that refuse to
hurry.
And I, I stand here in the way
to beg you with my eyes — *"just look at me,*
know me and remember
pink Cadillac rides through skyscraper cities."
We felt that we could fly.
You rode Blackjack to claim the blue ribbon,
the crowd was wild.
You smelled of faroff shores —
I would be just like you one day
with bracelets of golden ballerinas and Parisian tokens,
with soft brown hair and leather sandals in every color,
with laughing voice and elusive ways,
diamond sprinkled fingers,
pink nails perfect half moons in the sky.

And so I understand, I understand.
You came and went but always came again for me,

until now.

Mamma's House

Her house burned one night,
not exactly the fall of Atlanta or the Chicago fire,
but still it was a fire of some note
as photographs of dead sons and one daughter
arched and curled and ended.

Her favorite overstuffed chenille chair
became a skeleton in seconds.
Her green and yellow McCoy
cracked and blistered away.
Her painting of sailing ships
listing to the left,
placed at the foot of Mama's bed so that
she could look first thing in the morning
before rising and say to herself,
"When my ship comes in,
there will be changes around here,"
became part of the ravaged remains.

Pots and pans and caramel candy
and a secret stash of Coca Cola
were rendered useless somewhere
between 10:00 and 11:00 — a little before
the witching hour.

The family peering from the Ford LTD,
arrived in a rush, careened crazily onto the lawn
between the crepe myrtle and the water hydrant,
watched this proud woman pace,
stop and turn soundlessly in circles,
cry without tears, scream without voice,
as firemen buried the last of her children
and linens and fine lace and lifetimes away.

Mama stood in a faded cotton duster, without shoes,
stood and wondered how on earth
a heating pad, a little *Ben-Gay*
and an early death could take her by surprise
in this way.

Filigree

I lay these stones to rest
as surely as the child who placed the headstone.
I lay these stones to rest, gaunt tombs of evisceration,
lacerations that would not heal
the landscapes ever changing
but in some ways frozen
waiting for the Prodigal Son.
I carve these stones with my tears
and salt the earth with my grief.
I carve these stones with a jagged knife
and shape these jewels with my life.
They tear into my flesh as it falls away
in cascades of blood and luminosity —
petals bursting into the earthly air.
The smooth gray stones, the cracks
yawning in the heat
and the nighttime terror—-

> flowers
> growing
> gracing
> these graves
> knowing
> that the
> gardener
> is only
> late
> in
> coming.

Metronome

He came like a suitor to tell me you were leaving on this day.
(I knew he never liked you anyway.)
He came bowing, cavorting, searching for a cap
to still his pretty hands while nodding to himself
in false humility.
He told me stories of his deaths — a brother who died,
a mother soon to follow.
Art really is imitation after all.
He came like a postman, self-important with his certified letter,
with his time-laden talk, with his bag of secrets and scented rag
paper,
like a fugitive poet eager to spill my pearls and twist each strand
to choke the very life from me,
to examine my vertebrae like so many ivory keys,
my mind like so much refuse.

He came —
a barber shearing lives, meticulously, measuring in a mirror,
"we must have balance."
He came—
a watchmaker shaping time alone in apologetic rooms.
He came —
a butcher slicing sinew, separating form
from the ugliness of the reeking air —
blood screams its own tale forever,
a metronome of despair.

Fragile Fire

We invert the heart — it is a lonely trap
and a steep path down.
We crack the bowl and spill the sounds of joy
and lose this golden rope to cities in the sun.

It is a long way home.

We search a heart, a map of fire and fragile rememberings
basking in a shadow in a doorway down the lane
in a land we go to
when all else fails and fields no longer harbor us,
in a place away from lights lit for the night,
in a place where going is a blessing
and a curse.

A long way home.

Brides in Waiting

Brides in waiting,
step daintily among the juicy grass and thorns,
tread lightly upon the crest of earth and morning place,
sprinkle petals into an open mouth and feed
the crystal smile of hope.

Brides in waiting,
choose your colors well and adorn your bodies
like ornaments of hope.
Caress your arms and swan-like necks,
your spreading thighs and saucered hands,
sip from the barest smile an element of grace.

It is the least we can do.

Brides in waiting
cascade into the upturned air and lean into the day
a symphony of speech and song and youth and pride
and ageless mark of rage,
relentless in its beautiful ferocity.

Gentlest of Prisons

I grieve these places early
and with gusto
ranting out my ragged remorse
even as I spread
my soul in flight
toward the next place
I will be.
I grieve
the beloved faces
of so many landscapes
I have walked
so many trees
and mountain friends
and seasons stealing in
to quietly interlace
into the gentlest of prisons.

I grieve these places early
and smells of summer
marching toward conclusions
and of robins and of gulls
the rivers ever wild,
uncivilized and fragrant
lying at the feet
of doe and flowers and Fall.

I grieve these places early
adorned with faces
I have come to know
enchanted enemies of my dreams
wind chimes I will no longer hear
snows I will no longer feel
erasing my tears
even as they fall.

I grieve these places early.

Embroideries

The coming together
of twos—
two minds
two hearts
two wills
two loves
multiply
all the good
that is and that can be,
strengthened
as if forged in fires
of our own making.

The lives —
roots intertwined.

The smiles —
mysteries unraveled.

The words —
beatitudes

more beautiful
than we can fathom
embroidered
with pearls of faith,
rubies of hope,
and diamonds of charity.

Radiant Flight

I go drowning down around this craggy precipice,
this angular slope of steel and skin, myopic eye
of nighttime blue, sweetened with Summer's drop
of rain upon your concentrated brow,
glistening with your smile of innocence, of fallen grace,
silhouettes shaping themselves among slanted shadows
cast in corners where I stand observing,
poised to flee the radiant flight
of birds abreast, of skies aflame,
of love unknown, of love unclaimed.

Sweet Surcease

The open palm of desire
begs an audience, a moment, a passing glance.
Caress me before the touch,
breaths apart, heat hovering in the yearnings
of your beautiful eyes, depths I go down, down into.
Shadows silken on my shoulders, settling into memory
even as I reach for you,
your mouth a pathway, gates guarding treasures beyond trespass.
Let us relearn each truth in delicate detail,
crucifixions of the Soul,
the baptism by fire and chariot's rush,
the standing alone to stand together,
the pain and sweet surcease of struggle.

Harbor Home

I will abide here
in my heart
with you.

I will shelter here
in desert tents
of strength and silk.

I will talk with you
through evening winds
and lightning skies
and darkest times.

I will dream you
alone and sacred,
proud and profane,
I will dream you.

I will pleasure you
with secret voices
and jeweled smiles,
with echoes dancing
in oases dark.

Silhouettes shimmering
out of reach,
beckoning back
to quietest rapture,
to passion's cry,
to love most rare,
to harbor home,
to shelter
here,
I will abide
With you.

Niagara

In the light and the dark, I will come to you,
a water dance upon the eaves,
a crystal tear among the waves,
a quickening beat upon the breast of night.

And I will beckon you to me

with spinner's wheel and solitude
and sails aburst with flame
with smiling eyes and shyest glance
a storm's Niagara of wildest dance
of light and dark and child's unfettered play
among the elements of deepening day —

at once naive, at once alive, at once,
at last the truthful binding
of worlds within as worlds collide,

laments hanging in the reverent air
and gypsy scarves and caravans
departing for worlds unknown
prisms, lifetimes, smiles and touch
silent strife, the final struggle
of a well-lived life.
I will come to you.

Feast of Mourning

This mighty feast is spread before me,
delicate eyes beckon,
landscapes quicken beneath my touch,
mountains
 valleys
  chasms

to span amid sweetest rains and scented storms.
I would drown here as you look at me.
I would reach for you in complete faith,
in complete surrender —

but there are days to conquer
and false loves to exhume.
There are fears hidden even now
amid this mighty feast of
 mourning.

Swan

The swan in a gathering darkness
is a symphony, a madrigal,
a flute played at midnight
among mimosa and memories and trellises
and trembling constellations,
falling stars in an obsidian eye.

The swan in a gathering darkness
softness of dragon's breath
smoke a velvet coat to waft and weave,
the two-stringed lyre
the funeral pyre
siren song of immortality
and God's hand gently placed
in final acknowledgment
of our spent journeys, our spent youth,
the coming home to rest
upon smooth sheets of mountain water
and the quietness of a waiting place,
the well known face of a gathering darkness.

Angels Abounding

We are here, all angels abounding
privileges precise, prosaic within
the filtered light of cathedrals dim
peopled with shadows and greater selves.
The halting cry of passion spinning out its fruit
along darkened corridors
and destinies deplete against revisions
of the soul.

We are here, all angels abiding,
newness claimed before the start of frenzy
music sweet in a distance,
incantations chanted with incense and spiraled sighs
and Loon's song billowing down
around the feet to softly settle
like a cat upon the hearth,
to curve into the hollows of our hearts,
and then to drape the shroud of so many
fallen saints, of these angels,
we angels abounding.

A Round . . .

The World will come around again
and bless me with its quietness
and quintessential platitudes,
pools of wisdom mirroring in the forest medieval minds.

The World will come around again,
the humming bird, the dappled egg,
the quiet death
and dying life.

The World will saunter past my window
pulling with it promises of a youth untouched
and words unspent, ablaze with all the waiting
 of a tear upon the lash.

The howl and whimper, the bursting forth in song of light,
in song of primal things
and wings of strength to hold us up
The world will come around again.

Sudden Details

Jim Walker

When you get right down to it
the building blocks are the same,
but the products, the meanings, if you will,
evolve from sudden details of timing.

Writing is pretty much all process. Beyond the act and process of
writing is just nice conversation.

Nice conversation (without *trying* to sound arrogant); to my
mind good poetry echoes and touches some chord of human
experience. There are things all people, share on a common ground
of empathy. The rational tools of poetry allow folks to better
communicate more than what words alone are able to do; to make a
good poem is to evoke what just words or rhythm cannot. And I
don't think this is an easy thing to do, I certainly don't achieve it as
often as I would like, but I love finding it as a writer, reader or
listener.

Leaving

Stop don't move,
I want to remember you
before I go back to my small rooms,
my uncertain light . . .

Look at yourself   touch yourself,
the curve and design of you,
the tug and release of muscle
in your rising to the mirror
in the hunger of the body
to savor every moment

of what we lay hands on
or put words to,
in this steady desperation
of leaving

if we don't rise —
or at least try to . . . please,
come here or   don't   move

For A.

Once I said memory doesn't matter
after its center has disappeared,

but now —*note: mention here the details*
I can no longer see clearly, or rest in

the colors of, some small things
both of us may have touched

or called attention to, even just for a moment,
when our perceptions became indivisible —

you are gone, dead, buried,
and my memories are little,

they are like abandoned torchbearers

wandering every direction, fully aware
of the approaching cool and heavy night

but unsure what this means for them,
what to do with such knowledge.

So Much, So Much, Oh . . .

Passion 2   for Tara

A man builds a birdhouse
every year for his daughter,
eighteen this morning
along the posts of his fence
where an agreement of birds
sings evening's light,
each year more songs
surround this house
which silence grips.

A private woman kept
a financial record
for sixty-eight years.
Her marriage starts with a loan
of forty dollars to a bachelor,
her children are accounted for,
each one a little less than the last;
but before all this, in the beginning,
"slot machine, 3 plays & glass of wine,
two dollars and fifty cents won."

What is the color for
becoming a way of making?

And over here, a young couple
just months married in a new house,
his family's ocean fishing town house,
as he is a fisherman
and she a fisherman's wife;
they have reconciled with struggle
and own the whole of their hearts
and the sea-wrecked moon ripples
in through the bedroom window

and nothing may separate them.

And for the older couple, grandchildless,
shoving furniture around at midnight
for the move in the morning,
the power flickers and fails;
he in the front bedroom, she in the kitchen.
Oh, how they called out and reached out
through a dark maze of the familiar,
lamp stands and slipcovers, edges and corners,
hips faltering on each brass-nailed armrest
not suddenly in its place,
oh, how they found each other hearts racing,
breathless, whispering, *it's ok, it's ok, it's ok*

What is the gesture for *yes*,
we leap from brilliant tragedies
so much so, so much so, oh . . .

or the sound for
the empty space inside the bed

or the weight on your shoulder of the touch
no, don't leave, I, I, . . .

The Birthday Trampoline

for a girl off Hwy. 84

The blue vinyl presses hot and almost sticky against her hands and the back of her legs. The smell of the new cut prairie and southern breeze swirl away under the grind of the interstate. She steps to the middle of the trampoline as the ground forgets her. The springs quietly hush, pulling the fading dark blue fabric taut, like a lake in a postcard, or the thin blue of horizon at the beach, and vaguely, her mother and father off to the side, like flat stones, *money, no, I don't understand you, I got a deal, we can't, but, but,* quietly she begins to bounce, not jumping, her hair and arms bobbing, she glances at her feet and then south, toward town oh *my god, the money, you, we can't, you, jesus christ, but look* now bending her knees a little, enough for air to push under her feet, the sky always stretches huge and blue here, it's her secret with everyone *couldn't you just, money, think, a good idea, the money, we don't have, but look, honey, look,* a little higher each time, knees slightly bending, bare arms out and skinny hips swaying for balance, she sees farther every time she rises, the roof of the house slopes away brown and rough, the interstate growls on the ground, the wind tastes warm and sea-like, and so clear *we don't have, why, my god, a good idea, can't you, you never think, oh jesus* now she rises more than she falls, over town, and Dallas, and New Orleans, and the Gulf Coast like a long spoonful of blue with a wave rolling through forever oh, *how many times, I'm sorry, I'm sorry, but, honey, honey look at her* the waves never stop rolling, no matter what, and they're a blue hollow inside and the sky throws blue everywhere and she touches the bottom of the sky — lightly — it is just as she imagined, she smiles and giggles *oh my god, my god, where is she going, oh my god, holy jesus shit what, get my baby down, oh bye honey, bye-bye, please, oh bye-bye* she forgives the need to want to go down, she swoops up the wind and heads southeast, the smell of straw and old earth falling away, the blue air wrapping her in coolness and from here, she knows, everything plays on pure desire.

The Coach

His ex-wife reaches for their daughter. He kneels,
glancing back at the field through a rush of leaves,
turns and looks down and away. A thin line breaking
the sidewalk catches his eye, a familiar one
he knows has grown wider since last season.
He tries to remember how it got this far
without someone trying to fix it, patch it up, smooth it over.
She's in the car, having nothing more to say, but he,

he thinks she should try. He expects her to try. His daughter
watches him through the window's reflection of his breath
catching in his throat. Their taste of autumn will be this
plain sadness and loss of quiet words, the good words
hidden in separation. He stands, stretches against his collar,
waits as they drive away . . . as evening settles back on him
the playing field, other responsibilities, other passions,
where the light is strong and another season beginning.

As Much As Any Two People

Outside the hospital on a Friday morning a man holds his head
down against his knees with his hands as our coffeeshop words
drift past him, already tired themselves. The sun breaks then
and slowly lights the trees before settling across his shoulders.

This scene resembles others,
you could say they come
a dime a dozen, or
once in generations.

Neruda cradled kisses and ruined men
dearly and equally, a yin-yang
as much as any two things.

And this man holding his head outside the hospital,
light seems to have its own love for him,
inflaming him, entangling the interrupted facts
of his hands slipping from the hours of a Friday morning.

Perhaps he's terminal or just losing his mind,
perhaps there's a woman involved, hurt, in trouble or
laughing somewhere, maybe there's nothing more
to be done, and all that can be done is to wait.

Mr. T. Ryan sang, "And it's hard
to miss a kiss, my friends,
but such a harder thing
to miss the risk. . . "

Sometimes you do pay with your life. You just do.
Surrender or embrace, our greetings and departure,
escaping, dancing, those sudden details of timing.

To wrap up:
more sugar?

How do we end this? You and I?
How did I know you this morning?
Who is that man running toward us?

Smoldering

for us

A long coolness of shadow falling
through downtown at the lunch hour rests
on intersections, next to barber shops,
underfoot and in fists clutched in pockets.

Meanwhile, a woman
in a creased, sharp, black dress
blindly patrols the meadow
where highway seventy-one used to run
keeping her head lowered;
telephone lines guide her north,
her hands hang loose,
light consumes everything.
Desperation, however short-lived,
can break you.

Paint "Figure on Highway in Meadow,"
with turquoise sky and hunching grass,
sparks of green, blue, orange, other golds
circling the fragile off-center blockish round sculpture
of a shawled, no, a tight-wrapped old woman in light
black, something dragging in the dirt from her hands.

Unable to forget the lady in this new painting,
or the almost great presence of light in their city,
people topple into their passions, fighting harder
to endure beautiful strangers, their monthly debts,
lovers, friends dying. *How have we survived*
this long with so much love and grief and work
without any destination in mind? Friend, be startled by yourself
in an evening window scaling the depths, think all at once:
The Fire Rages Out of Control — Figure on Highway in Meadow.

Dinner Napkin as Icon

Left behind, the creased rage of the inside
of a fist untwists on a couple's table,
some deep measured silence
loosening to what it was, unresolved.

We will arrive at the edge of another bed,
expectations in hand, unable to think anymore
the struggle is hopeless. Your time, too, is coming.

      Eat well and have sex
as much as possible, so much time goes wasted
just weighing the pros and cons of things
devoured whole vs. left untouched, unopened.

A dog hair can split the wind.
Passion lends itself to use, once claimed.
Are you still here? Do you need a tissue?

Memory Study 2

Open, please . . . wider, wider, good . . .
shut the eyes before they turn on the light,
don't watch their fingers curling down
close . . . open . . . wider . . . a little more
water hardly takes the thick soap off their fingers
or the tang from the metal picks, the taste from the mouth
close . . . open . . . close . . . open, please . . .
close . . . open . . . close . . . open & wide
leaning over, one by one, then one by one again
a history of poor attention . . . open . . . close . . .
open . . . close, good . . . open . . . close, close, thank you
only know two of them, the rest seem to have read the file

yes, this whole area of instability . . . close . . .
soon — tune out — fall asleep — they're doctors,
with a patient with a problem, and such common hopes
and close . . . no, the mother is outside . . . close, please . . .
open . . . close . . . open, wider . . . wider, good
the specialist from Stanford has come for a look
under the plastic bib protecting the nice clothes
open . . . close . . . open . . . close, please . . .
good . . . open . . . close . . . close, thank you
these are indeed, however, the most comfortable chairs in the world
open, open. . . let me see the anterior . . . open, wider . . .

sleep, don't hear the specialist wiggle the incisors, then the bicuspids,
murmur into the chasm behind the pre-maxillary segment
good, close . . . open . . . close . . . open, please . . .
or the dentist ask which restaurant is good for everyone
or the stranger dig around the impacted wisdom teeth
good, close . . . open . . . close . . . open, please . . .
or another stranger use his fingers to show the first stranger
how and where a palatial expander might really be a viable option
good, close . . . open . . . close . . . open, please . . .
it's alright not to ask, it's expected, they are doctors after all,
they have clean tools and photos, a timeline and sometimes
close . . . open . . . close, thank you . . . open . . .
surrender is easier
close . . . open . . . wider . . . a little more . . . good,
close . . . now open, wider, yes, as wide as you can . . .

Listening to Poets

for H.

Once, she leaned over, glancing
at his closed mouth as if surprised
to find it on his face. Then,
brushing his arm, with her hair just bobbed so
it couldn't drift and stay on his shoulder and also
smelling of baked apples . . she leaned closer,
letting her breath slip out in a delicate slice
across his earlobe and neck, the intimate warmth
of an unclosed wound, "I can't trust anyone here
to read my eulogy." Then she leaned back,
her bare lips kissing each other closed.

Weaving

Passion 1

Pulling flowers from their jars
gathers time like a stone
to a hidden heart.

Pulling flowers from their jars
separates beauty
from any one thing.

He slits the sweet fruit
not missing a beat,
knife dipping out and in
and back around again
until all that is left
is what he needs.
Explain yourself
in the voice of cutting.

She is released from smoke
in a fresh choreography
of forgetting the way home.
Smoothly, she moves so
hands tumble back to tables,
purposeless.
Have no doubts
in the pause in a motion.

Pulling flowers from their jars
bundles us together
like twigs, like a photo album.

You could live where I live, and love
the procession of days this same way,
but everyone knows this. So how
do we keep missing each other?

Even in the desperation of leaving,
the relentless faith in her eyes
and the fine arguments of his hands
distract them from their last hopes
they could move on from here
unfettered with each other's gifts.

Pulling flowers from their jars
raises every fact
most like breathing.

We could save each other and forget
to escape, to slip away from what
we have seen held in our hands.
A hapless content would find us,
and home we would all go,
warnings tucked in pockets.

Look, those two above, they are drowning
in the desire and terror in silence -
of things continuing without them;
they strain against the world quietly,
ready to surrender everything
if only asked, if only told they could.

Pulling flowers from their jars
gathers us around the fire
of our unsuspecting light.

Pulling flowers from their jars
rebuilds familiar shelters
with a single-minded trust.

After Living with Someone

Here is what we've worked out so far:

Luck is the moment you recognize
preparation just meet opportunity.
Let me also include the color of the sky,
the height of the windows, the season,
and the way someone listens, listens
to nothing in particular at all.

Spring winds and the rain they bring
arrive quickly, as if almost late,
vanish into the garden together
and lose even themselves,
as if each were promised
only to the waiting seeds.

One night you will save me:
my door will be unlocked
and as I hear you coming
I'll pretend to be sleeping
and running from wolves;
I won't tell you this.

We are ever pulled down
by the science of being here;
by why we can walk here easily
but not on any moon
or shouldering any more life
than our own for very long.

All day I've been wondering
if it could rain again,
or when you would break
and call me in for lunch.
All day I've been working,
on small things quietly waiting.

The world works this way too,
but with a thin prescience,
lacing one detail into the next,
with no need of a clear design
but only of a tightening pattern;
no place can remain just as it was.

Overture

Passion 3   for Ralphie

No, wait, here, this is what I mean:
the great song is not so important
as a moving dancer, that evidence

of low notes folding together
the corners of a round heart
with great care and without caring.

Ok, but in another world,
not once removed in elegance,
things will often break

and pause in a gray light;
which could have a weight,
and still spill through the air

and against your hand,
warm your palm
and be gone.

Yes, songs end, and your mind flies off
to shadows like swifts to a chimney
one night like a blue curtain rising

on some familiar rock bottom story.
Hey, don't stop dancing now,
we've almost made it.

You see how the pieces come together,
how these are the laws, and even you,
the consumate professional,

are a human being, and can be
just another terrified animal
just doing what you have to do

to be who you are, dancing some crazy jig
through your dark and echoing rooms.
I'm sorry, what were you saying?

As Regards

Chaos 1

Water, chapel tower, a fishing grizzly's paw

When you get right down to it
the building blocks are the same,
but the products, the meanings, if you will,
evolve from sudden details of timing.

syllables, boysenberries, stalking the wild

The child's cursive *lazy dog* dipped
through the dotted red and blue lines
as he fell to watching two pale geckos
curled under a honeysuckle's shadow
out on the brick window ledge.

fluency, robin's egg blue, our border war

Refuse to stop. This is evolution.
What remembers you? Your children, certainly,
your words, yes, your actions, of course.
Have you none of these? The pattern of your life
will find a design, like the wind does.

The perfect hope of a thing
discovers a shape unique
from magical details.

No, wait, everything falls into place
somehow, on its own,
let the children find the sense in it,
they will have their own anyway.

loaded gun, seed husk, the shallows
of light in the curve of her shoulder

Up the phone wire outside my door
ivy vines climb, hung with cicada skins
outgrown and forgotten, how long
has this been going on?

The vines slowly climb up a white wire
to twirl in sunlight with their desire.
Crickets and stamens rising in season
oh fly me, oh fly me right on to heaven.

This vine, this . . .
breeze and steady
ecstasy.
What else matters but the effort?

our thin hands, oceans, how to have fun

Refuse to stop. You may be a revolution.
What remembers you? Everything.
Should I believe? Yes, yes.

Regarding the Return of an Average Man

They all waited a long time. When it was known he would return, they continued waiting, only then in heightened expectation, as if for a gathering storm heading down the coastline or like zealots for Judgment. People were seen stammering in their houses like caged horses or stretching to peer around corners and down long roads where the light held their lives each for a moment. A small, constant wind tossed loose scraps of the world around their feet; the heated, wet smell of juniper and broken presence of limestone waited with them and made the air heavy in their bodies. People ate quietly, slept and made love carefully, not afraid, but burdened with waiting for the news of their inevitable dreams.

In this way people set cups down lightly, with almost no sound, spoke to each other even more softly, held their own hands as if gauging the weight of their bones, quick lights flashing from their eyes, almost invisible. They each, in their time, made arrangements, wrote a few letters, decided what they could say to him.

Understand, the one they waited for is not a religious minded individual. In this case, it happens to be a man, but it never has to be. In this case, he is just a man people could devote themselves to easily, in spite of themselves. Imagine him as the hometown boy who left only to realize everyone else's dreams. Imagine him as someone you lost.

But when he arrived, he was not the man remembered, nor the man expected. He induced neither surprise nor relief, nor even disappointment. He sat down apart from them asking no one for anything, calling no one's name to sit beside him although he knew them all. In this way they all remained, with the sun setting far away and the quarter moon rising.

About the Writers

Valerie Bridgeman Davis grew up in central Alabama, nourished by the piney woods and storytelling tradition of her family. She moved to Texas in 1981. She earned a B.A. degree from Trinity University in 1986 and M.Div. degree in 1990 from Austin Presbyterian Theological Seminary, where she won the Charles L. King Preaching Award. Currently, she is completing a Ph.D. in Religion at Baylor University, works as a professor at Huston-Tillotson College, and as a part-time chaplain for Hospice Austin. She also serves Banah Full Community Church as a pastor, is a community activist, and mothers her teen-aged sons Darius and Deon. In 1995, she won the Austin Book Award for her collection, *In Search of Warriors, Dark and Strong, and Other Poems*. She is married to her partner and best friend, Don.

Lana Book is a graduate of Angelo State University. She is a registered nurse and currently works in an inpatient Hospice unit. Lana is a member of the Austin Writer's League and a weekly critique group, Quill Merchants. Her children's stories appear in each publication of the Cowboy Country Express. She lives in Kerrville, Texas at the Hill Country Sculpture and Meditation Garden, and has three grown daughters, her "shining stars."

Donna Woodard worked in the fields of public relations as a nationally accredited communicator, has taught at the university level at the University of Denver and now works in the emerging field of work force development in her home state of Texas. Perhaps the most special things in her life, however, are the birth of her daughter Katharine and the sharing of her "voice" through these poems.

Jim Walker grew up in Oregon, received Bachelors degrees in Creative Writing and Computer Science from the Univ. of Redlands before ending up in Austin. He got involved with local poetry open mikes and organizations fairly quickly and is a strong proponent of the spoken and written word as proactive arts. Currently he is a graduate student in Regional Planning at the Univ. of Texas at Austin, focusing on solid waste.

Susan Bright is author of fourteen books of poetry, three of which (**Far Side of the Word, Tirades And Evidence Of Grace** and **House of the Mother**) have been recipients of Austin Book Awards. She is the editor of Plain View Press which for the twenty-one years between 1975 and 1996 has published one-hundred-twenty books. She has edited the Plain View Press **New Voices Series** since 1986. **Coming Full Circle** is the tenth book in the series.